# This Secret Diary belongs to:

Nancy Clancy: My Secret Diary
Text copyright © 2015 by Jane O'Connor
Illustrations copyright © 2015 by Robin Preiss Glasser
All rights reserved. Manufactured in China.
www.harpercollinschildrens.com
ISBN 978-0-06-284660-0
Typography by Jeff Shake
19   BRR   10 9 8 7 6 5 4 3 2
❖
First Edition

# NANCY CLANCY
## My Secret Diary

Based on Nancy Clancy

written by Jane O'Connor

Cover illustration by Robin Preiss Glasser

**HARPER**
*An Imprint of HarperCollins Publishers*

# Bonjour!

If you're like Nancy, you are filled with stupendous, creative ideas. Here in your very own private diary, you can write all about your life, your friends, your family, or anything else you might fancy. And remember, this diary is one hundred percent confidential. (That means it's for your eyes only.)

Write your signature (your name) in the box below. Then decorate it in your own style.

## This Diary Belongs to:

# Essential Facts about Yours Truly:

I am _____ years old.

My birthday is _____.

I am in _____ grade.

I have _____ hair

and _____ eyes.

Other essential facts about me:

_____

_____

_____

_____

_____

| Plain | Fancy |
|-------|-------|
| Yellow | Gold |
| Leather | Patent leather |
| Glasses | Sun glasses |

_____

_____

# Lights! Camera!
# Picture time!

Nancy is always stylish or chic, as the French say.
That means she always looks her best. Draw a
picture or paste a photograph of yourself at your
most chic on this page.

# Fancy, Festive, Fun!

Nancy loves anything fancy, including lace fans, butterflies, and croissants. What are some of your favorite things? Draw them on these pages. You can use lots of colors, some sparkles, and stickers!

# All in the Family

Nancy's family prefers to dress casually. (That's a polite way of saying their clothes are plain.) But she still thinks they are absolutely stellar. Write about your family here.

My mom's name is _____.

My dad's name is _____.

I have _____ brothers and _____ sisters.

Their names are _____

_____.

A fancy word to describe my family is _____.

One fancy thing I do with my family is _____

_____

_____.

My favorite thing about my family is _____

_____

Draw a picture of your family, or paste a photograph of all of you together.

# Sensational Sister

*Nancy's younger sister is JoJo. She is a lot of fun—most of the time!*

What are some fun things that you like to do with your sibling(s)?

# Sibling Pastimes

JoJo loves doing anything with Nancy. Some of their favorite activities together are having beauty days, stargazing, baking cookies, and exploring in their backyard.

Draw a picture of what you like to do with your sibling(s).

# Keep Out, *S'il Vous Plaît*

As much as Nancy loves her sister, sometimes she wants some alone time.

## What do you like to do when you are by yourself?

Do Not
enTer
THIS
meANS
You
JoJo!

Draw your own Keep Out sign here.

# Mon Amie
## (that's French for my friend)

Nancy's best friend is Bree. She is the same age as Nancy, and she lives right next door. Write about your best friend here.

My best friend is _____.

My best friend is _____ years old.

I met my best friend when I was _____ years old.

When I first met my best friend, I thought _____

_____

_____

_____.

We knew we were destined (that's a fancy word for

meant to be) to be best friends when_____

_____

_____

_____.

Draw a picture or paste a photograph of your best friend on this page. Write some words around it that describe your friend. For example, for Bree, Nancy would write that she is "fabulous," "adventurous," and "intelligent."

# Artsy or Adventurous?
## Fancy Friend Facts

Nancy and Bree like to do many of the same things—making arts-and-crafts projects, having parties, and solving mysteries.

What are some favorite things you do
with your best friend?

_____

_____

_____

_____

_____

_____

_____

_____

_____

_____

_____

# Trading Secrets

When Nancy and Bree want to share secret messages, they write their notes in code and then send them in their Top-Secret Special Delivery mailbox. (This is a basket on a rope that hangs between their bedroom windows.) Do you and your best friend have your own secret language or a special way of communicating with each other?

## Nancy and Bree's Secret Code

| | | |
|---|---|---|
| A = C | J = L | S = U |
| B = D | K = M | T = V |
| C = E | L = N | U = W |
| D = F | M = O | V = X |
| E = G | N = P | W = Y |
| F = H | O = Q | X = Z |
| G = I | P = R | Y = A |
| H = J | Q = S | Z = B |
| I = K | R = T | |

Write a top-secret message to your best friend using their code!

* ❋ ❀ ❋ ❋

# Hush Hush Message

A secret message just for you is hidden in the puzzle below. Cross out the words "Nancy and Bree" every time they appear below to find out what Nancy wants to ask you. Write the message you have found in the puzzle on the lines below.

NANCYANDBREEWILLNANCYAND

BREEYOU NANCYANDBREEJOIN

NANCYANDBREENANCYANDBREEOUR

NANCYANDBREE SECRETNANCY

ANDBREECLUB?NANCYANDBREEOUI

ORNANCYANDBREENON?NANCYANDBREE

_____

_____

_____

_____

# Prized Possessions

Which of your possessions (possessions
are things you own) are very important to you?
Why are they so special?

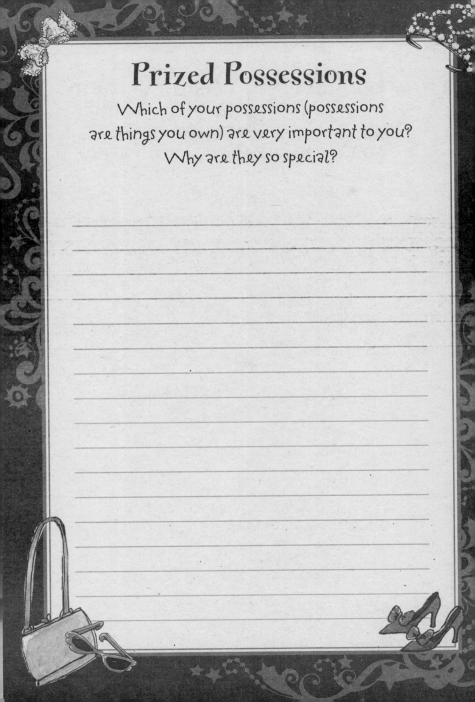

# Disastrous Disagreement

Sometimes Nancy and Bree have disagreements.
When friends argue, sometimes it can lead to hurt feelings.

Have you and your best friend ever had an argument?
If so, what was it about?

_____

_____

_____

_____

_____

Did you tell your friend why you felt
the way you did?

_____

_____

_____

_____

_____

_____

_____

_____

## How did you make up?

_____

_____

_____

_____

_____

_____

_____

_____

_____

_____

_____

_____

_____

_____

_____

_____

_____

_____

# Canine Companion

Nancy's dog is named Frenchy. Do you have a pet?

My pet's name is _____.

My pet is _____ years old.

My pet's favorite things are _____

_____

_____

_____

_____

_____

_____

Draw a picture or paste a photograph of your pet here.
Be sure to include some fancy accessories.

Nancy can't remember back when she didn't have a sister. But sometimes she wonders what it would be like to be an only child.

Are you an only child?

_____

_____

What is the best thing about it?

_____

_____

_____

_____

_____

_____

_____

_____

_____

_____

Do you ever wish you had a brother or sister?

_____
_____
_____
_____
_____
_____
_____
_____
_____
_____
_____
_____
_____
_____
_____
_____
_____
_____
_____

# Marvelous Marabelle

Nancy's favorite doll is Marabelle. She has beautiful hair and many fancy outfits. She sleeps in a canopy bed.

Do you have a favorite doll,
stuffed animal, or toy?

_____

_____

Does it have a name?

_____

When and where did you get it?

_____

_____

What is your favorite thing
to do together?

_____

_____

Draw a picture of you and _____.

# Reigning Queen

Sometimes Nancy dresses up and imagines she is a monarch. (That is a fancy word for king or queen.) Do you dream of being royal? Write your name on this crown and decorate it any way you like!

If you could be a queen for a day,
what would you do?

_____

_____

_____

_____

_____

_____

_____

Who would be in your royal court?
It could be your family, friends, or people you've
never met—like celebrities.

_____

_____

_____

_____

_____

_____

# Extraordinary
# Explorer Crossword

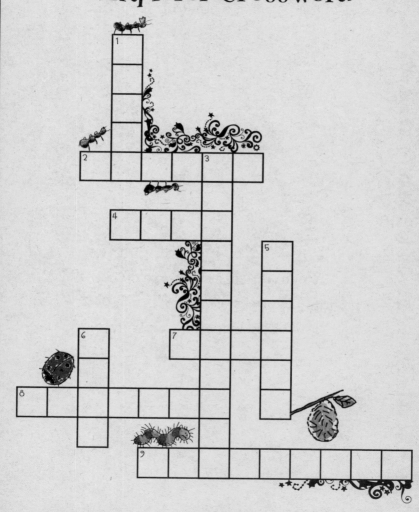

## Across

2. The scientific word for bug
4. Where baby birds live before they can fly
7. An animal with feathers and small bones
8. A type of rise in the ground that ants make
9. The cocoon that a caterpillar spins around itself

## Down

1. The head ant (or leader) that lays all the eggs
3. A wormlike creature with many legs that changes to become a butterfly
5. An eight-legged critter with no wings or antennae
6. An insect similar to a butterfly, but with plain brown wings

## Solution:

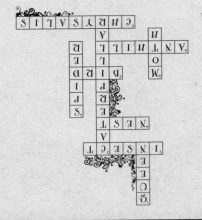

# Updo, Anyone?

Do you ever imagine yourself with a completely different hairstyle? What would it look like? Draw it in the frame.

Sophisticated

Swanky!

...unty!

Glamorous

Diaphanous

Radiant

Whimsical

# Stepping Out

Sometimes Nancy's family goes out for dinner at the King's Crown.

### What restaurant is your favorite?

_____

### Who do you go with?

_____

_____

### What do you like to eat there?

_____

_____

_____

### What do you wear when dining out?

_____

_____

# Etiquette Word Search

When dining out, it is important to follow the rules of etiquette (that means good manners). Nancy likes it when people use French words like merci or when they call each other "darling." Find these words in the puzzle and circle them.

MADAME          DIVINE

SIR             DAPPER

DARLING         HOSTESS

MERCI           RSVP

PARDON          LOVELY

| T | O | O | N | F | O | A | E | M | Z | X | M |
|---|---|---|---|---|---|---|---|---|---|---|---|
| H | O | S | T | E | S | S | J | E | H | A | A |
| H | W | P | A | R | D | O | N | R | B | X | D |
| L | D | N | M | E | H | O | N | C | Q | T | A |
| D | A | R | L | I | N | G | D | I | A | E | M |
| V | P | S | O | L | O | V | E | L | Y | E | E |
| S | P | V | L | J | R | L | I | T | B | K | N |
| P | E | P | M | K | S | D | I | V | I | N | E |
| Z | R | K | R | N | I | U | B | F | X | N | N |
| D | T | S | W | O | R | N | P | X | U | O | M |

Solution:

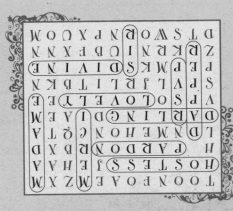

# Festivities

Nancy loves the holidays. For Christmas, her favorite pastime is decorating the tree with her family.

### What is your favorite holiday tradition?

_____
_____
_____
_____
_____
_____
_____

### Do you have a favorite ornament or decoration?

_____
_____
_____
_____
_____
_____
_____
_____
_____

ornaments

Who do you visit around the holidays?

_____

_____

_____

_____

_____

_____

_____

What is your favorite holiday memory?

_____

_____

_____

_____

_____

_____

_____

# Dream Getaway

Nancy can't wait to get a passport, which travelers need to go abroad (that means to another country). She yearns to go to Paris.

## Where would you most like to travel?

_____

_____

_____

_____

_____

_____

_____

_____

_____

_____

_____

_____

_____

_____

_____

_____

Plan an itinerary for your trip! That's a fancy word for schedule.

_____
_____
_____
_____
_____
_____
_____
_____
_____
_____
_____
_____
_____
_____
_____

# Travel Log

I have traveled to these places: _____

_____

_____.

My favorite vacation was _____

_____.

The people I most like to travel with are _____

_____.

When I travel, I like to bring _____

_____.

My fanciest travel memory is _____

_____

_____.

# Remember Me

A souvenir is something that reminds you of a special place. At the beach, Nancy likes to take home seashells as souvenirs.

What souvenirs have you collected from your trips and adventures?

_____

_____

_____

_____

_____

_____

_____

_____

_____

_____

_____

_____

# What kind of traveler are you?

Take this quiz to find out.

1. Which location would be your dream vacation spot?

a) a lake or a beach with white sand, an umbrella, and maybe a hammock

b) a city filled with beautiful parks, restaurants, and museums

c) a mountain with a zipline or a tropical island where you can snorkel

2. Your luggage usually contains:

a) just the essentials: a change of clothes, a toothbrush, and a travel scrapbook. Do you like to travel light so you can explore at a moment's notice?

b) lots of books, swimsuits, extra sunglasses, a hat, and a nice, big towel to relax on. Do you prefer to chill out?

c) You can never be too prepared: hiking shoes, a backpack, kneepads, Band-Aids, swim goggles, and trail mix

Seaside Inn

3. If you could stay at any hotel in the world, you would want it to have:

a) an amazing ice cream parlor, a cool museum nearby, and awesome city views

b) those cute little bottles of creams and soaps. You like to turn your hotel room into a relaxing spa experience! Also, a lazy river would be fun!

c) a waterslide and a really high diving board

4. You bring home a souvenir from your trip. It is most likely:

a) Pretty stones and seashells you collected on the beach

b) a collection of postcards from an art museum to frame and put on your bedroom wall

c) Who has time for souvenirs?! You were too busy practicing cannonballs from the high diving board.

5. You're about to dig into a fabulous meal.
   What's on your plate?

a) something you can hold while you're on the go. Probably a sandwich or yummy pastry from a local café

b) a huge omelet with cheese. You need energy to get through your action-packed day.

c) a picnic lunch on your beach towel, or french fries and a burger from the hotel snack bar so you can get back to snoozing or reading

6. What kind of shoes are you wearing?

a) flip-flops

b) comfortable shoes for walking miles and miles

c) gorgeous hot pink ballet flats

7. You have just arrived at your destination.
   What is the first thing you do?

a) put your suitcase down and quickly look up the nearest theme park or water park

b) You don't even bother heading to the room because there is a zoo nearby with a great penguin show!

c) jump on the hotel bed to see how soft it is. Then soak in the Jacuzzi.

8. Your family and friends tend to describe you as:

a) a curious person who is always up for trying something new

b) a homebody who likes to take it easy

c) a go-getter who seems to never get tired and loves a challenge

Now add up your points to find out your score.

## Point Key

| | | |
|---|---|---|
| 1. A) = 1 | B) = 2 | C) = 3 |
| 2. A) = 2 | B) = 1 | C) = 3 |
| 3. A) = 2 | B) = 1 | C) = 3 |
| 4. A) = 1 | B) = 2 | C) = 3 |
| 5. A) = 2 | B) = 3 | C) = 1 |
| 6. A) = 1 | B) = 2 | C) = 3 |
| 7. A) = 3 | B) = 2 | C) = 1 |
| 8. A) = 2 | B) = 1 | C) = 3 |

GRAND TOTAL= _____

### Beachcomber (8–13 points)

An ideal vacation for you always includes water, sand, sun, and plenty of relaxing. You prefer daydreaming, reading, and watching the clouds to seeing the sights. Your perfect vacation spot would be anywhere with a beach, lake, or pool, and warm breezes.

### City Slicker (14–19 points)

You love, love, love going to museums, the theater, and restaurants. Your ideal vacation includes visiting a zoo, science museum, or seeing a circus or musical, and of course, lots of ice cream. Cities are your perfect vacation spot, because you like exploring and being on the go.

### Great Adventurer (20–24 points)

You are the first person on the longest water slide. Your favorite vacation includes lots of physical activity like hiking, zip-lining, skating, or bodysurfing. You are happiest near a beach with great waves or a mountain resort with tons of outdoor activities.

# Classy Classroom

Nancy makes her school days fancy, whether it's by dressing up with her whole class or bringing a fancy pen with a plume to write with.

**What do you do to make your school day festive?**

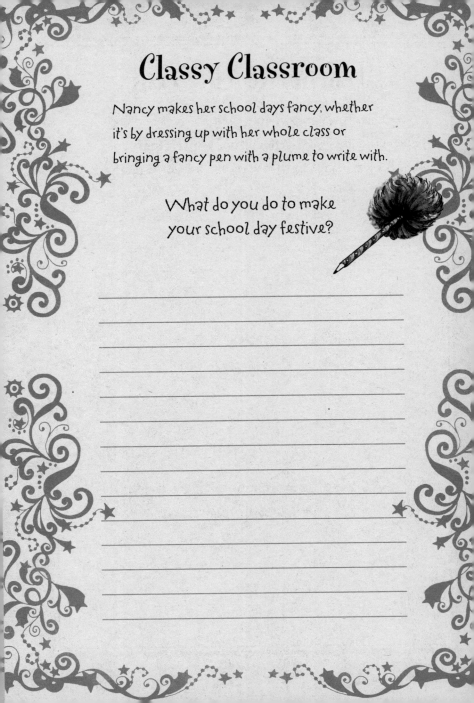

_____

_____

_____

_____

_____

_____

_____

_____

_____

_____

_____

# Teacher of the Year

Mr. Dudeny is Nancy's third-grade teacher. He always comes up with superb activities and projects for Nancy and the kids in her class. Do you have a favorite teacher?

## What makes your teacher so amazing?

_____

_____

_____

## Has this teacher taught you something you never knew about?

_____

_____

_____

## What was the most memorable thing your teacher did with your class?

_____

_____

_____

_____

# Cool School Memories

At family day at Nancy's school, kids get to show off some of the great projects they have been working on. Does your school have a family day (or something like it)?

Who came to see you that day?

_____

_____

_____

_____

What project or presentation were you most proud of? (For example, it could be a poetry reading, a play, or art projects.)

_____

_____

_____

_____

_____

_____

_____

_____

What does your school look like?

_____

_____

_____

_____

What's your school's name?

_____

Draw a picture of it here:

# Hostess with the Mostess

Have you ever dreamed of throwing the ultimate fancy party? Who would you invite? Write their names here. (P.S. They do not have to be people you actually know. You could invite the president or your favorite author. It's your party!)

_____

_____

### What would the theme of the party be?

_____

_____

### What kind of food would you serve?

_____

_____

_____

### What would you wear?

_____

_____

_____

# Party Planning

Sometimes when Nancy is planning a party, she likes to go through magazines for inspiration. (That's a fancy word for something that helps you get great ideas.) Cut out some pictures from magazines or newspapers that inspire you to plan the best party ever.

# Party Word Find

Nancy wants to be the best hostess ever. Below are some items Nancy thinks are essential to throwing a great soirée (that's a fancy name for an evening party). Find these words in the puzzle and circle them.

UTENSILS          STREAMERS

CANDLES           TIARAS

PLATTER           BOUQUET

SAUCERS           DOILY

CONFETTI

```
K D X Y G S T R Y C A H
C P Y Z M T I P B A P S
O L O Q J R A S O N B J
N A S K L E R T U D X S
F T D A W A A R Q L V A
E T O G G M S N U E B U
T E I R T E H W E S L C
T R L Z K R A C T K V E
I B Y P R S C V L I B R
D U T E N S I L S M Y S
```

Solution:

# Post-Party Memories

The best party I've ever been to was _____

_____.


_____ invited me to the party.


My favorite memory from this party is _____

_____

_____

_____

_____

_____

_____.

Draw a picture or paste a photograph of yourself at the party on this page.

# Career Opportunities

Nancy is not sure what she'll be when she grows up.... An explorer, an artist, a poet perhaps? Or someday she may open a detective agency with Bree!

### What do you want to be when you grow up?

_____

### Do you know anyone who has that job?

_____

_____

### What do you hope to accomplish in that job?

_____

_____

_____

_____

_____

_____

_____

Sleuth Headquarters

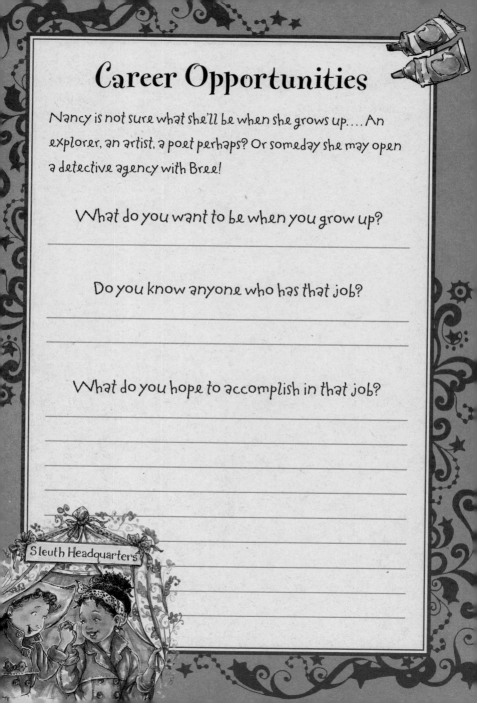

# Hidden Talents

Nancy's neighbor Mrs. DeVine used to work at a hair salon as a beauty care professional.

## Are there any people you've known for a long time with a special talent or interesting profession?

_____

_____

## What did they do?

_____

_____

_____

## What do they do now?

_____

_____

## How did you find out about their talent or past career?

_____

_____

# The best thing that happened to me this week was . . .

_____

_____

_____

_____

_____

_____

_____

_____

_____

_____

_____

_____

_____

_____

# Sweet or Salty

Sweet, salty, or a little of both? Take this quiz to find out which of these flavors makes your taste buds zing! Circle one answer for each question.

1. When I go to the movies, I must have:

a) buttered popcorn

b) jelly beans

c) ice cream!

2. My favorite after-school snack is:

a) cheese and crackers

b) a peanut butter sandwich

c) trail mix with salty nuts, chocolate pieces, and dried fruit

3. My mom made me the best lunch!
In my lunch bag I have:

a) a turkey-and-cheese sandwich, some chips, and a pickle

b) a yogurt with cut-up berries, granola, and a banana

c) a bagel with cream cheese or hummus, and a fruit cup

4. My friend has my favorite snack in her lunch bag.
I'm going to trade her my:

a) carrots for her salty nut mix

b) sliced cucumber for her chocolate chip cookie

c) crackers with cheese for her apples with cheese

Now add up the number of
a's, b's, and c's you picked.

How many a's? _____
How many b's? _____
How many c's? _____

## If you picked mostly a's:

You are a Salty Sailor. You love savory tastes (savory is fancy for salty), from chips to nuts, to yummy cheese.

## If you picked mostly b's:

You are a Sweetie Pie! You love your sweet treats, from cookies to strawberries. Just make sure you brush your teeth often!

## If you picked mostly c's:

You are a Mix Master. You like to blend savory and sweet tastes together for the ultimate flavor combinations.

# What's on the menu?

People in France love to eat snails. In French, that's escargots (ess-car-go). Have you ever tried a new food that you weren't sure about at first, and then you were surprised at how good it tasted?

### What was it?

_____

### What made you try it?

_____

### What is the most exotic food you have ever tried?

_____

### What did it taste like?

_____

_____

### Is there any food you have tried that you would absolutely never try again?

_____

_____

# Stellar Stargazer

One of Nancy's favorite things about summer is camping out in the backyard. Nancy and her dad like to make a fire and roast marshmallows while they gaze at the stars.

### Have you ever gone camping?

_____

### Was it in your backyard or somewhere else?

_____

_____

### Who did you go camping with?

_____

_____

_____

### What did you like best about camping?

_____

_____

_____

Was there anything you didn't like
about camping?

_____

_____

_____

_____

Did you spot something in the sky you might not have
seen if you hadn't been sleeping under the stars?

_____

_____

_____

_____

_____

What was it?

_____

_____

_____

_____

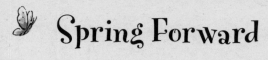

# Spring Forward

Nancy looks forward to spring because that is when Mrs. DeVine's flower garden is in bloom.

### What is your favorite season?

_____

### Why do you like this season the best?

_____
_____
_____
_____
_____

### What kinds of activities do you enjoy doing most during this season?

_____
_____
_____
_____
_____

Do you enjoy seeing the seasons change, or would you prefer just one to last all year?

_____

_____

Why?

_____

_____

_____

_____

_____

_____

What season is it right now?

_____

Are you having fun, or are you hoping for the weather to change?

_____

_____

_____

# Plié Please

Nancy teaches her dad what she's learning at ballet school. He tries his hardest, but ends up in a tangled mess during their first lesson. Have you ever had a friend or family member agree to do something they were not very good at, but they did it anyway because they are good sports?

### What activity was it?

_____

### Did you help that person improve (that's fancy for get better)?

_____

_____

_____

_____

### How?

_____

_____

_____

_____

# Most Improved

At the end of their ballet lesson, Nancy gives her dad an award for being most improved. Draw an award for someone you know who tried his or her best at something difficult.

# Members Only

Nancy and Bree are founding members of their very own club (founding members means they started the club).

Do you and your friends have a special club?

_____

_____

_____

What is it called?

_____

How does someone become a member?

_____

_____

_____

What does your club do?

_____

_____

_____

_____

# Headquarters

Nancy and Bree love to meet in their clubhouse
to discuss important club matters.

## Where is your clubhouse?

_____

_____

Draw what it looks like. (If you don't have a clubhouse,
imagine the coolest clubhouse you can and draw it here.)

# This week the best thing that happened to me was . . .

# Dream *Boudoir*

From her canopy bed to her enormous hat collection,
Nancy's *boudoir*—or bedroom—is a fancy dream come true.
And she created it herself!

### What are some things you absolutely love about your room?

_____

_____

_____

### Do you ever wish you could redecorate your room?

_____

How would you change it?

_____

_____

_____

_____

_____

Draw a picture of your dream room.

# Goal Keeper

Many of the kids in Nancy's class play on soccer teams. Nancy thinks this is the best sport because so many kids can play in a game.

### What is your favorite sport to play or watch?

_____

_____

_____

### What position do you play?

_____

### If you could be like any athlete when you grow up, who would you choose? Why?

_____

_____

_____

_____

_____

# The best thing that happened to me this week was . . .

# Spa Day

A day at a spa is one of the most glamorous ways to spend time. Nancy treated her mom to an all-expenses-paid afternoon at the Ooh La La! Beauty Spa, conveniently located in the Clancy's backyard. From the spa menu below, design your perfect spa getaway by circling the services you would like to include.

DELUXE HAIR CARE

FACE MASK

MANICURE

MASSAGE

PEDICURE

TOTAL MAKEOVER FOR A NEW YOU!

Who would you take to the spa?

_____

_____

_____

_____

_____

What would you do after your beauty day?

_____

_____

_____

_____

_____

_____

_____

_____

_____

_____

_____

_____

# Chilling Out

At the spa, you are supposed to think relaxing thoughts.
Sometimes it helps to visualize (that means to picture in your
head) places or things that make you feel relaxed (like ocean
waves, or cuddling a pet, or raindrops falling). Cut out pictures
from a magazine that you find relaxing and paste them here:

# Mood Swings

Sometimes Nancy feels glum (that's another way of saying down in the dumps), or exasperated (fancy for frustrated), or anxious (which means nervous).

### Have you ever felt this way?

_____

_____

_____

_____

_____

_____

_____

_____

_____

_____

_____

_____

_____

_____

_____

## What made you feel better?

# Laughter Is the Best Medicine

When Nancy throws Frenchy a birthday party, all the dogs go crazy, and Nancy ends up with cake all over her favorite dress. But everyone around her starts to giggle; Nancy can't help giggling too. Have you ever been upset, but then something happened to make you feel OK again?

## What frustrates or angers you the most?

_____

_____

_____

_____

## What's the best way for someone to cheer you up?
## (For Nancy, it is other people laughing.)

_____

_____

_____

How do you get over a tense or stressful situation?
Deep breaths? Counting to ten?

_____

_____

_____

_____

_____

_____

_____

_____

_____

_____

_____

_____

_____

_____

_____

_____

_____

_____

# The best thing I did
# this week was . . .

# Bibliophile

Nancy is a bibliophile—that means she loves books.

Do you enjoy reading?

_____

What are your favorite books?

_____

_____

_____

_____

_____

_____

_____

_____

_____

_____

_____

_____

_____

Who is your favorite character from a book?

_____

_____


What would you say to that character if you
met in real life?

_____

_____

_____

_____

_____

_____

_____

_____

_____

_____

_____

_____

# Aspiring Author

Nancy has made up a character named Lucette Fromage who is nine years old and has incredible adventures. Do you ever think about becoming a writer?

What kinds of stories would you tell?

_____

_____

_____

_____

_____

What would your main character be like?

_____

_____

_____

_____

_____

Can you think of a good title for your story?

_____

_____

Start your story! If you get writer's block—which means you don't know what should happen next—ask a friend to help you get creative with some brainstorming!

_____

_____

_____

_____

_____

_____

_____

_____

_____

_____

_____

_____

_____

_____

_____

# Role Model

One of Nancy's role models is her teacher, Mr. Dudeny.

## Who is someone in your life you admire?

_____

_____

_____

_____

_____

## How did you meet?

_____

_____

_____

_____

_____

_____

_____

_____

_____

## What do you admire most about him or her?

_____
_____
_____
_____
_____
_____
_____
_____

## Why do you want to be like him or her?

_____
_____
_____
_____
_____
_____
_____

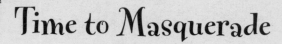

# Time to Masquerade

Nancy adores Halloween because it is all about dressing in costume (or masquerading). What was your favorite Halloween costume?

### Where do you go trick-or-treating?

_____

_____

_____

### Who do you go with?

_____

_____

_____

_____

### What is your best Halloween memory?

_____

_____

_____

_____

Draw a picture of your favorite costume.

# Secret Admirer

On Valentine's Day, Nancy and Bree try to match up two teenagers. Have you ever had a secret admirer? Have you ever sent someone you like a special unsigned card or present?

If you had a secret admirer, did you figure out who it was?

_____

How did you feel after you discovered who your secret admirer was?

_____

_____

_____

_____

Is there someone you would like to send a Valentine's Day card to?

_____

Are you too embarrassed to send it?

Instead, you can draw your card here.

# Unofficial Holiday

Sometimes just for fun, Nancy likes to make up her own unofficial holidays, like when she celebrated Jackson Pollock Day and invited her friends to put on an art show. If you made up a holiday, what would you call it?

## How would you celebrate the holiday?

_____
_____
_____
_____
_____
_____

## What would you wear to the celebration?

_____
_____
_____
_____
_____
_____

Draw a special card for this holiday.

# On Your Toes

Nancy and Bree attend ballet class every week. Nancy can't wait to be able to dance *en pointe* (that means dancing on your toes).

### Do you like to dance?

_____

_____

### What kind of dancing do you enjoy?

_____

_____

_____

_____

_____

_____

### Do you take dance classes?

_____

_____

_____

# Time to Curtsy

Have you ever been on stage?

_____

_____

_____

What was it like performing in front of
your family and friends?

_____

_____

_____

_____

Were you nervous?

_____

_____

_____

_____

_____

_____

# The best thing that happened this week was . . .

# Inspiration Is Everywhere

Nancy admires the paintings of Claude Monet, who liked to paint outdoors—even in winter! Find a spot outside, or look out a window, and draw what you see.

# SWAK!

Nancy adores getting mail. Sometimes when Bree writes a letter to Nancy, she writes SWAK on the envelope. That means "sealed with a kiss."

### Do you like sending letters and notes?

_____

_____

### Who do you send letters to?

_____

_____

_____

_____

_____

_____

### On what occasions do you send letters?

_____

_____

_____

# Love, Nancy!

Write a letter to Nancy!
What secrets will you share with her?

_____

_____

_____

_____

_____

_____

_____

_____

_____

_____

_____

_____

_____

_____

_____

_____

_____

_____

_____

_____

_____

_____

# Star Light, Star Bright

Nancy and JoJo know that you can wish on the sun, because it is a star, after all.

Do you ever make wishes on stars or throw a penny into a wishing well?

_____

_____

_____

_____

_____

_____

_____

_____

_____

_____

_____

_____

_____

_____

_____

_____

# What do you wish for?

Look outside your window at night and draw a picture of what the moon looks like.

# Night Sky Constellations

Nancy's dad shows JoJo and Nancy the constellations in the night sky. Constellations are groups of stars that make a picture like a connect-the-dots puzzle.

Draw your favorite constellations.

# Somewhere over the Rainbow

Nancy thinks rainbows are magnificent.

Have you ever wondered what is at
the end of a rainbow?

Write about it on the lines below, and then draw a picture of it.

_____

_____

_____

_____

_____

_____

_____

_____

_____

_____

_____

_____

_____

_____

# Roses Are Red . . .

In school, Nancy takes a survey of friends' favorite poems. (A survey is when you ask a bunch of people some questions and write down their answers.)

## Do you have a favorite poem?

## What is it?

# Violets Are Blue . . .

Compose (that means write) a poem of your own. If you need inspiration, just do what Nancy does, and turn on some music.

# This One's for You!

When you write a poem to someone special, it is called an ode.

## Who would you write an ode to?

It can be someone you know or someone you've never met, like your favorite author or musician. Write an ode to someone who's inspired you or someone you appreciate a lot.

_____

_____

_____

_____

_____

_____

_____

_____

_____

_____

_____

_____

_____

_____

_____

# Funny Faces

Whenever Nancy is in a photo booth, she makes lots of silly faces. Have you ever been in a photo booth? What kinds of faces did you make? Draw them below.

# (Not On) Speaking Terms

Nancy loves her little sister, but sometimes JoJo makes Nancy so angry she refuses to speak to her.

Have you ever been so mad at someone that you stopped speaking to them?

_____

Why were you so angry?

_____
_____
_____
_____
_____

How did you forgive that person?

_____
_____
_____
_____
_____
_____

# Legendary!

Nancy's dad likes to make up stories too. He once told her about the legend of the Diamond Tiara. It is about a beautiful princess named Nanette who falls in love with a commoner (that is someone who isn't royal).

What is your favorite legend or fairy tale?

Draw the story here.

If you were the star of your own fairy tale,
what would happen? Write about it here.

# Most Stupendous
# Birthday Ever

Write about the most stupendous birthday party you ever had.

The best birthday party I ever had was my _____ birthday.

My party was at _____
_____
_____
_____

It was stupendous because _____
_____
_____
_____
_____
_____
_____
_____

# Greetings and Salutations!

Nancy enjoys chatting with her grandpa on the phone.

## Who are your best phone pals?

_____
_____
_____
_____
_____
_____

## What do you like chatting about?

_____
_____
_____
_____
_____
_____
_____
_____
_____

# Fantasy Phone Call

If you could call anyone famous, who would it be?

_____

_____

_____

_____

What would you want to ask?

_____

_____

_____

_____

_____

_____

_____

_____

_____

_____

_____

# On the Move

Nancy likes to stay active. That means she is always on the move. She likes Hula-hooping, dancing, playing soccer, and exploring the outdoors.

### What physical activities do you do to get your heart pumping?

_____
_____
_____
_____
_____
_____

### What would you like to learn to do?

_____
_____
_____
_____
_____
_____

# Tea for Two

Bree has a tea set made of real china (not plastic). It was a present from her aunt. Bree's mom and aunt used to play with it when they were young girls.

Has a relative ever given you something special?
What was it?

_____

_____

Do you use it often?

_____

_____

Is there something of yours that you
think you would like to give to someone else
once you are a grown-up?

_____

_____

_____

_____

_____

# Forget Me Not!

Nancy loves any excuse to celebrate, so she keeps a calendar of important occasions—birthdays, holidays, anniversaries.

## What occasions are on your calendar?
### Make a list of them here.

_____

_____

_____

_____

_____

_____

_____

_____

_____

_____

_____

_____

# Fabulous and Fancy Me!

Some words to describe Nancy are "glamorous," "imaginative," and "thoughtful."

What are some words that best describe you?
Write down as many words as you can think of
(the fancier, the better!).

_____

_____

_____

_____

_____

_____

_____

_____

_____

_____

_____

_____

_____

_____

_____

_____

# The best thing that happened this week was . . .

# Applause, Applause!

Nancy is so impressed that you have finished your diary! It is a huge accomplishment. Write a note here about what you hope to accomplish when you are older. Later you can look back at this diary and see how far you have come!